RED RIDING HOOD

Retold and Illustrated by

JAMES MARSHALL

SCHOLASTIC INC.

New York Toronto London Auckland Sydney

To Joseph Bryans

ISBN 0-590-44991-5

Copyright © 1987 by James Marshall.

All rights reserved. Published by Scholastic Inc., 730 Broadway,

New York, NY 10003, by arrangement with Dial Books for Young

Readers, a division of Penguin USA.

12 11 10 9 8 7 6 5 4 3   2 3 4 5 6/9

Printed in the U.S.A.   08

First Scholastic printing, December 1991

A long time ago
in a simple cottage
beside the deep, dark woods,
there lived a pretty child
called Red Riding Hood.
She was kind and considerate,
and everybody loved her.

One afternoon
Red Riding Hood's mother called to her.
"Granny isn't feeling up to snuff today,"
she said, "so I've baked
her favorite custard
as a little surprise.
Be a good girl and
take it to her, will you?"
Red Riding Hood was delighted.
She loved going to Granny's—
even though it meant crossing
the deep, dark woods.

When the custard
had cooled, Red Riding Hood's
mother wrapped it up
and put it in a basket.
"Now, whatever you do,"
she said,
"go straight to Granny's,
do not tarry,
do not speak
to any strangers."
"Yes, Mama,"
said Red Riding Hood.

Before
long
she was in
the
deepest
part
of
the woods.
"Oooh,"
she said.
"This is scary."

Suddenly a large wolf appeared.
"Good afternoon, my dear,"
 he said.
"Care to stop for a little chat?"
"Oh, gracious me,"
 said Red Riding Hood.
"Mama said not to speak
 to any strangers."

But the wolf had *such*
 charming manners.
"And where are you going,
 sweet thing?" he said.
"I'm on my way to visit Granny,
 who lives in the pretty yellow house
 on the other side of the woods,"
 said Red Riding Hood.
"She's feeling poorly,
 and I'm taking her a surprise."
"You don't say," said the wolf.
 Just then he had a delightful idea.
 No reason why I can't eat them *both*,
 he thought.
"Allow me to escort you," he said.
"You never know what might be
 lurking about."
"You're too kind," said Red Riding Hood.

Beyond the forest they came
to a patch of sunflowers.
"Why not pick a few?"
suggested the wolf.
"Grannies *love* flowers,
you know."
But while Red Riding Hood was
picking a pretty bouquet,
the clever wolf hurried on ahead
to Granny's house.

"Who is it?"
  called out Granny.
"It is I, your delicious—er—
  darling granddaughter,"
  said the wolf
  in a high voice.
"The door is unlocked,"
  said Granny.

"Surprise!"
cried the wolf.
Granny was furious at
having her reading interrupted.
"Get out of here,
you horrid thing!"
she cried.

But the wolf gobbled her right up.
He didn't even bother to chew.
"Tasty," he said, patting his belly,
"so tasty."
Just then he heard footsteps
on the garden path.
"Here comes dessert!"
And losing no time, he put on
Granny's cap and glasses,
jumped into bed, and pulled up the covers.

"Who is it?"
  he called out
  in his sweetest granny voice.
"It is I, your little granddaughter,"
  said Red Riding Hood.
"The door is unlocked,"
  said the wolf.

Red Riding Hood was distressed
at seeing her grandmother so changed.
"Why, Granny," she said,
"what big eyes you have."
"The better to see you, my dear," said the wolf.
"And Granny, what long arms you have."
"The better to hug you, my dear," said the wolf.
"And Granny, what big teeth you have."

"THE BETTER TO EAT YOU, MY DEAR!"
cried the wolf.

And he gobbled her right up.
"I'm so wicked," he said. "*So* wicked."
But really he was
enormously pleased with himself.
And having enjoyed such a
heavy meal, he was soon snoring away.
A hunter passing by was alarmed
by the frightful racket.
"That doesn't sound like Granny!"
he said.

And so the brave hunter
jumped in the window,
killed the sleeping wolf,
and cut him open.
Out jumped Granny and Red Riding Hood.
"We're ever so grateful,"
said Red Riding Hood.
"That wicked wolf won't trouble
you again," said the hunter.
"It was so dark in there I couldn't read a *word*,"
said Granny.
Red Riding Hood promised never,
ever to speak to another stranger,
charming manners or not.

And she never did.